Hello, Family Members,

Learning to read is one of the most [illegible] of early childhood. **Hello Reader!** [illegible] children become skilled readers who like to read. Beginning readers learn to read by remembering frequently used words like "the," "is," and "and"; by using phonics skills to decode new words; and by interpreting picture and text clues. These books provide both the stories children enjoy and the structure they need to read fluently and independently. Here are suggestions for helping your child *before*, *during*, and *after* reading:

Before

- Look at the cover and pictures and have your child predict what the story is about.
- Read the story to your child.
- Encourage your child to chime in with familiar words and phrases.
- Echo read with your child by reading a line first and having your child read it after you do.

During

- Have your child think about a word he or she does not recognize right away. Provide hints such as "Let's see if we know the sounds" and "Have we read other words like this one?"
- Encourage your child to use phonics skills to sound out new words.
- Provide the word for your child when more assistance is needed so that he or she does not struggle and the experience of reading with you is a positive one.
- Encourage your child to have fun by reading with a lot of expression . . . like an actor!

After

- Have your child keep lists of interesting and favorite words.
- Encourage your child to read the books over and over again. Have him or her read to brothers, sisters, grandparents, and even teddy bears. Repeated readings develop confidence in young readers.
- Talk about the stories. Ask and answer questions. Share ideas about the funniest and most interesting characters and events in the stories.

I do hope that you and your child enjoy this book.

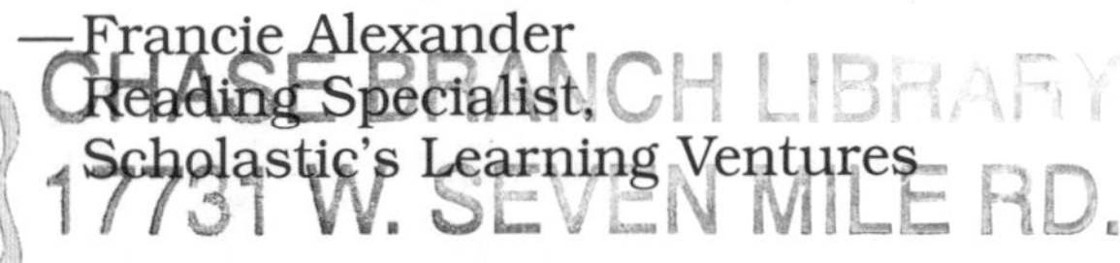

—Francie Alexander
Reading Specialist,
Scholastic's Learning Ventures

For Ripton Gruss Rosen
—K.M.

To Edie Weinberg, art director extraordinaire
—M.S.

ISBN 0-439-20673-1

Library of Congress Cataloging-in-Publication Data available

10 9 8 7 6 5 4 3 2 1 01 02 03 04 05

Printed in the U.S.A. 24
First printing, March 2001

by Kate McMullan

Illustrated by Mavis Smith

Hello Reader!—Level 3

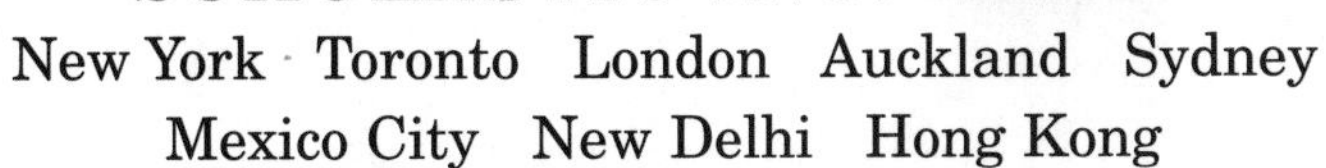

SCHOLASTIC INC.

New York Toronto London Auckland Sydney
Mexico City New Delhi Hong Kong

What's For Lunch?

Ms. Day's class
was going on a field trip.
Everyone was rushing around,
getting ready to go.
No one gave Fluffy his lunch.

Emma picked Fluffy up.

"We are going to the planetarium,"

she told him.

"We are going to look at the stars."

Stars, schmars, thought Fluffy.

What's for lunch?

"Line up!" called Ms. Day.
Jasmine ran over to Emma.
"Come on," she said.
"Let's sit together on the bus."
Emma put Fluffy down.
The girls hurried off.

Fluffy sniffed.

Mm-mmm, he thought.

I smell something yummy.

Fluffy followed the yummy smell.
It led to Ms. Day's purse.
Fluffy saw keys.
He saw some money.
He saw a big red apple.
Lunch time! thought Fluffy.
Fluffy dove into the purse.
He took a bite of the apple.
CHOMP!
He took another bite.
Yum, thought Fluffy.
I love lunch!

AVE'S
R REPAIR
55
-6071
appl
milk
bread
tooth
butte
sauce
etti
cat food

All of a sudden
the purse started swinging.
Whoa, there! thought Fluffy.
He held onto the apple.

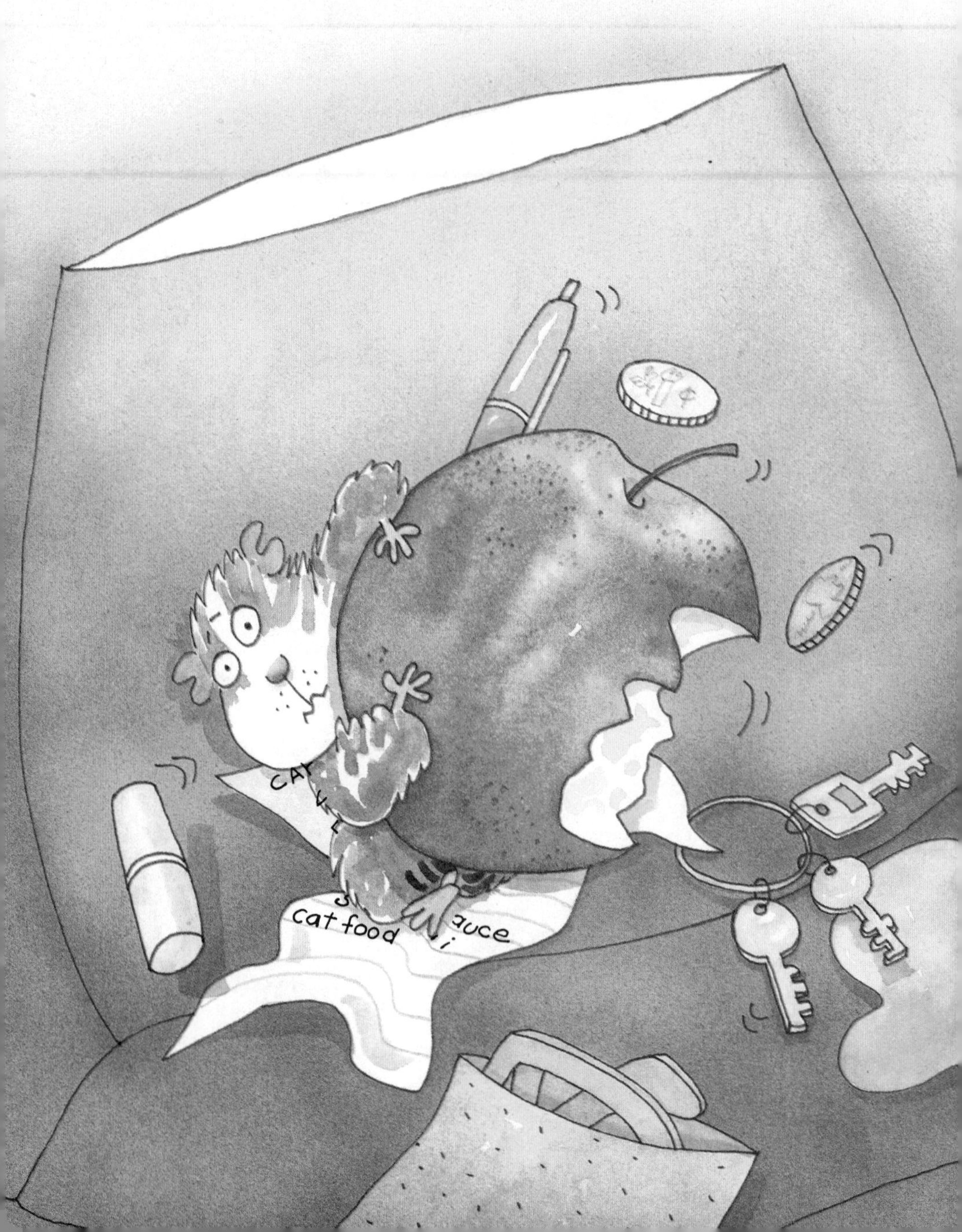

Fluffy rocked this way and that
inside the purse.
His lunch rocked this way and that
inside his tummy.
Ugh! thought Fluffy.
Get me out of here!

At last the swinging stopped.
Fluffy heard an engine start.
Where am I? he wondered.
He heard Ms. Day say,
"You may eat your snacks now."

A hand reached into the purse.
It picked up the apple.
Hey! thought Fluffy.
I'm not finished yet!

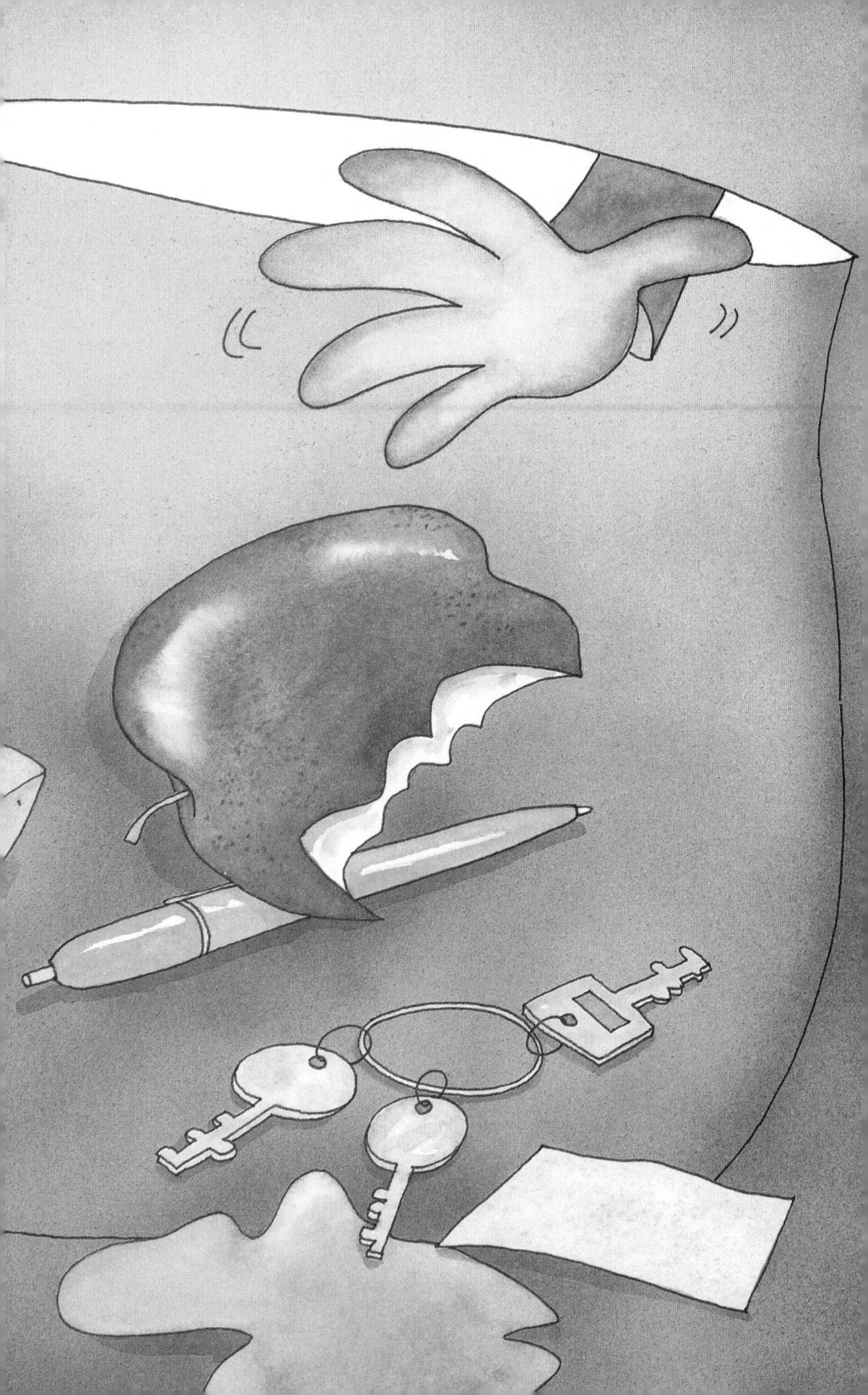

“Eew!” said Ms. Day. “My apple!”

***Your* apple?** thought Fluffy.

I don’t think so.

Ms. Day picked Fluffy up.
"Fluffy!" she said. "I can't believe
you hid in my purse!"
I can't believe
you stole my lunch,
thought Fluffy.

"I'll take care of Fluffy, Ms. Day,"
said Emma.
Ms. Day gave Fluffy to Emma.
She gave her what was left
of the apple, too.

Fluffy quickly finished
the apple.
"Now you can look at the stars
with us, Fluffy," said Emma.
Stars, schmars, thought Fluffy.
What's for dessert?

Fluffy Sees Stars

Ms. Day led her class
into the planetarium.
Everyone sat down.
Emma held Fluffy on her lap.

Slowly, it began to grow dark.

Hey! thought Fluffy.

Who turned out the lights?

A loud voice said,
"Welcome to the night sky!"
Yikes! thought Fluffy.
Who said that?

"What if there were no stars?" said the voice. "The night sky would look like this."

Like what? thought Fluffy. **I can't see a thing.**

"But the night sky is filled
with stars," said the voice.
Stars popped out
all over the sky.
Everyone said, "Oohhhh!"

“Long ago, people in Greece saw these same stars,” said the voice. “They thought some groups of stars looked like pictures. Star pictures are called constellations.”

All I see are a bunch of white dots, thought Fluffy.

“It is not easy to see
star pictures,” said the voice.
No kidding, thought Fluffy.
“These lines may help you,”
said the voice.
Lines connecting the stars
appeared in the sky.
“That looks like a giant
connect-the-dots puzzle,”
Emma told Jasmine.

“This is the constellation Pegasus,”
said the voice.
“Pegasus is a horse with wings.”
You call THAT a horse?
thought Fluffy.

“The Greeks used long-handled
ladles to dip water,” said the voice.
“They called this constellation
the Little Dipper.
That one is the Big Dipper.
Can you see the handle?”

“I see it,” said Jasmine.

“Me, too,” said Emma.

“Do you see it, Fluffy?”

Oh, sure, thought Fluffy.

But he didn’t.

Not really.

"The Big Dipper is part of a bigger
constellation," said the voice.
"It is called Ursa Major,
or the Great Bear."
Where? Where? thought Fluffy.
I can't see any Great Bear.

"The constellations move across
the night sky," said the voice.
Fluffy tried to see the star pictures.
But the dark made him feel sleepy.
Fluffy closed his eyes.
The voice kept talking,
but Fluffy didn't hear a thing.
Zzzzzzz, snored Fluffy.

The Great Pig

Welcome to the night sky!

Fluffy told the little guinea pigs.

Look hard!

You can see star pictures!

Where? We can't see anything! said the little guinea pigs. **Nobody said it was easy,** Fluffy told them. **Maybe some lines will help.**

This star picture shows
a flying guinea pig, said Fluffy.
We call this constellation
Pigasus.

Here is the Big Food Bowl.
Next to it is the Giant Carrot,
said Fluffy.
We see them! said the little guinea pigs.

This is the best constellation,
Fluffy told the little guinea pigs.
It is called Fluffy Major,
or the Great Pig.

Is it named after you?
asked the little guinea pigs.
Of course, said Fluffy.

In the sky,
the Great Pig ran over to
the Big Food Bowl.
The Great Bear showed up, too.
Back off! said the Great Pig.
This is my Big Food Bowl.

Grrr! growled the Great Bear.
We could share, said the Great Pig.

The Great Pig ran across the sky.
He picked up the Little Dipper.
He ran back to the Big Food Bowl.
Just one Little Dipper full?
asked the Great Pig.
Grrr! growled the Great Bear.
You win, said the Great Pig.

The Great Pig ran over
to the Giant Carrot.
He was about to take a bite
when Pegasus flew over.
Pigasus flew over, too.

Pegasus took one end of the
Giant Carrot in his teeth.
Pigasus took the other end.
They flew away with it.
Come back! cried the Great Pig.
Come back with my carrot!

"Fluffy?" said Emma.

"Are you having a bad dream?"

Huh? Fluffy woke up.

He was on the bus.

He was on Emma's lap.

"Did you like looking at the stars?" said Emma.

Stars, schmars, thought Fluffy.
What's for dinner?